W9-AQB-294

01/2018

Dear Parents:

Congratulations! Your child is taking the first steps on an exciting journey. The destination? Independent reading!

STEP INTO READING® will help your child get there. The program offers five steps to reading success. Each step includes fun stories and colorful art or photographs. In addition to original fiction and books with favorite characters, there are Step into Reading Non-Fiction Readers, Phonics Readers and Boxed Sets, Sticker Readers, and Comic Readers—a complete literacy program with something to interest every child.

Learning to Read, Step by Step!

Ready to Read   Preschool–Kindergarten
• big type and easy words • rhyme and rhythm • picture clues
For children who know the alphabet and are eager to begin reading.

Reading with Help   Preschool–Grade 1
• basic vocabulary • short sentences • simple stories
For children who recognize familiar words and sound out new words with help.

Reading on Your Own   Grades 1–3
• engaging characters • easy-to-follow plots • popular topics
For children who are ready to read on their own.

Reading Paragraphs   Grades 2–3
• challenging vocabulary • short paragraphs • exciting stories
For newly independent readers who read simple sentences with confidence.

Ready for Chapters   Grades 2–4
• chapters • longer paragraphs • full-color art
For children who want to take the plunge into chapter books but still like colorful pictures.

STEP INTO READING® is designed to give every child a successful reading experience. The grade levels are only guides; children will progress through the steps at their own speed, developing confidence in their reading. The F&P Text Level on the back cover serves as another tool to help you choose the right book for your child.

Remember, a lifetime love of reading starts with a single step!

For Peter, Laura, and Billy,
who always want a hug!
—A.S.C.

Text copyright © 2000 by Alyssa Satin Capucilli
Cover art and interior illustrations copyright © 2000 by Jim Ishi

Visit us on the Web!
StepIntoReading.com
randomhousekids.com

Educators and librarians, for a variety of teaching tools, visit us at
RHTeachersLibrarians.com

Library of Congress Cataloging-in-Publication Data
Capucilli, Alyssa Satin
Bear hugs / by Alyssa Satin Capucilli ; illustrated by Jim Ishi. — 1st Random House ed.
  p. cm. — (Step into reading. A step 1 book)
Summary: Baby Bear decides that of all the hugs from Mama and Papa Bear, a group hug
is best.
ISBN 978-0-307-26113-7 (pbk.) — ISBN 978-0-307-46113-1 (lib. bdg.) —
ISBN 978-0-307-51383-0 (ebook)
[1. Hugging—Fiction. 2. Bears—Fiction.]
I. Ishi, Jim, ill. II. Title. III. Series: Step into reading. Step 1 book.
PZ7.C179Be 2003 [E]—dc21 2002012965

Printed in the United States of America 37 36 35 34 33 32 31 30 29 28

This book has been officially leveled by using the F&P Text Level Gradient™ Leveling System.

Bear Hugs

by Alyssa Satin Capucilli
illustrated by Jim Ishi

Random House 🏠 New York

Mama Bear,
I want a hug!

A big hug?

A small hug?

A growing very tall hug?

Papa Bear,
I want a hug!

A wet hug?

A fly up to the sky hug?

How about a funny hug?

How about a honey hug?

A blackberry hug?

A blueberry hug?

A nose all red
with cherry hug?

How about a wiggly hug?

How about a giggly hug?

WAIT!

I know the hug
that's best for me.

It's a hug—
a hug for three!